Introductio

My name is Bobtor, I was once very bo
someone to choose me to come home
in, I knew straight away he needed me
important mission. I went home with him and he told my very important
job was to look after his friend Lou who was moving away from the Isle of
Wight to the mainland all by herself. His name was Big Rob.
He is called Big Rob because I'm Little Bob.

Turns out I have the best job in the world as for years Lou and I have
travelled and gone on amazing adventures and I am so lucky to have her
as my owner. My little brother William (who is bigger than me!) Came
along and we became inseparable. He is so cheeky if not a bit lazy and a
bit of a piggy when it comes to snackies!

Our friends loved our photos and stories of our days out so much we set
up our Bearygoodfun Facebook page and they encouraged me to try
writing a book!

We started cycling during the Covid-19 lockdown on our trusty bike
Bobby. We managed to cycle 1084 miles which is the distance from Lands'
End to John O'Groats. We did it all virtually as during lockdown you aren't
allowed to go outside but we still got a lovely shiny medal too.

Because we love cycling and the Isle of Wight so much, we decided we
needed a proper adventure and when the lockdown restrictions were
lifted and we were allowed we planned our trip and I wanted to share our
story with you.

Saturday 8th August 2020

Yippee, holiday time again. We have loaded up Bobby bike and he is fit to bursting mainly because of Williams snacks. We had to get up super early, but it is worth it as we get more holiday time. We hopped in our basket on the front of Bobby bike, William wriggling himself in position and putting on his lovely shiny red cycle helmet, I secured myself in my seatbelt. It is always a bit of a tight squeeze, but we jiggle about, so we get comfortable. It was so warm even at 7.30am. William put his sun cream on as he did not want his white stripes going red!

I am writing this from onboard the Red Funnel car ferry. Car ferries are great big boats that hundreds of cars can go on. There is even cafés and shops on board. We have got a great view as we have a seat by the window. We can see lots of little boats bobbing along in the water. The sails flapping gently in the breeze. The water is so beautiful and shimmery as the weather is gorgeous and so hot and there isn't a single cloud in the sky. The nasty corona virus is still about, and we all must be incredibly careful and to make sure we wash our paws and wear our masks. William is well chuffed as he has a new mask with "diddlies" (dinosaurs) on.

It is quite busy on the ferry today as like us, other children are now on school holidays too. Last time we came on the ferry we went outside but the weather is so hot we have decided to stay inside and enjoy the air conditioning!

Ooo we are docking, time to get on Bobby Bike again.

All Rights Reserved

This book is dedicated to the wonderful Robert Bailey for introducing me to my half pint pal, Bobtor.

And to the beautiful Kirsty Miller who completed the dream team with bringing home the barrel, William!

Cheers!

And special thanks to Paul Heal

We have just got to Nanny's house. Nanny lives in a town called Shanklin. It is towards the south of the island. We are staying at Nanny and Step Grampy's all week. Lou had barely unloaded our bags from Bobby Bike before William had found Nanny's stash of marshmoobles! He is sure that Nanny has got them in especially for him!

Our ride to Nanny's house was extremely hot as the sun is blazing and there is a heatwave! Sadly, the floating bridge is still broken so we did have to ride along the scary road through East Cowes but once we had made it to Island Harbour we were able to cycle safely along the Greenway into Newport. We like the floating bridge as its like a boat that gets pulled along by chains and takes you across the little bit of water between East Cowes where the ferry docks and Cowes where the Red Squirrel cycle route takes us all the way to Sandown. Going down the scary road takes us to join the Red Squirrel cycle route in the end, but the cars go so fast along the scary road, so we have to make sure we are being super safe and behaving ourselves.

It is worth braving the scary road as Its lovely going along the green way as its cool and shady and a nice fun ride. There is lots to see through the trees as you follow the River Medina and see lots of boats and birdies. We were so grateful of the shade from the trees. We go past a factory on the opposite side of the river that makes those giant windmills for windfarms. Its very clever, they turn wind into energy to power things. Good job they haven't seen how much wind William produces or he would have a full-time job.

As it was so hot, we had to make sure we drank lots of juice as we didn't want to get sun stroke and feel all poorly and get headaches from the heat. We are seeing Grandad later and want to make sure we are well enough for an adventure with him. William drank lots of juice, but It did make him need to tinkle so the last few miles were faster to try and get him to Nanny's in time, the sound of the river did not help! From Newport we followed our favourite Red Squirrel cycleway all the way through to Sandown and the last bit on the road to Nanny's house where William could finally uncross his legs! It's the best route as its nice and flat and a good surface for bobby bike. We can go fast enough to feel the breeze in our fur but we are safely away from cars and there is so much to see. Hundreds of trees and flowers, birds, over and under bridges. Every time feels like a different adventure as it looks different each time we visit especially as the seasons change.

William is hot and tired and doesn't want to go walking especially now that he has found the stash of marshmoobles I don't think we have any hope of him joining us. He reckons he is going to say in and "guard" them! He says he has a very safe place to hide them as he was patting his tummy!
Although it was extremely hot, I still really enjoyed my walk with Grandad We walked from Nanny and Step Grampy's house all along the cliff at Lake. I have walked that way before last time we came on holiday but today we walked even further and carried on all the way to Sandown. Lake is the little town between Shanklin and Sandown. I like walking along the cliff as you can look over and all the people on the beach look so teeny tiny like ants. Makes me feel like a giant!

When you look across from Lake cliff you can see Culver Cliff sticking out. Its white as it is made of chalk. When you look to the right you can see all the way along to Luccombe. Today we walked even further than last time I walked along Lake cliff and we carried on all the way to Sandown.

We walked past Sandown Pier and down along the beach to Yaverland. The beaches were busy, and it was lovely seeing people playing games like catch and swimming in the sea and enjoying the beach. There were some children burying their friends in the sand! That looks like fun! It would take me ages to bury William as his tummy sticks up quite high even when he is laid down! I really like going to the beach, but I don't like going in the sea. Making sandcastles is my thing!

At Yaverland there is the Zoo. I love the zoo and William and I have been there before, but it was too late in the afternoon to go today and we hadn't even had our picnic yet.

We walked up a great big hill and because it has been so hot all the grass was brown and dry, and it felt all crispy under my feet. It was hard work walking up the hill and we were all puffing and panting but we didn't stop. I'm glad we kept going as there

were amazing views when we carried on. We were so high up and we hadn't even made it to the top. Grandad said we didn't have time to go all the way to the top today, but he has promised he will take me all the way up to the monument one day.

We found a great place to lay out the yellow spotty blanket and have our picnic.

Our picnic was delicious. We had ham salad sandwiches, popcorn and a nice refreshing pot of sliced peaches. I spilt peach juice all over myself and got all sticky but luckily Lou always has wipes with her because of William's many spills! I just hoped the wasps didn't sniff me out. We had started to head back down the hill after our picnic, it is so much easier going back down than it as walking up. It felt like we came down a lot faster too!

When we got down to the seafront at Sandown we stopped to have a refreshing ice lolly as the sun is still as hot as an oven If only William was here. He will be so disappointed that he has missed out on an ice lolly mind you he is probably stuffed full of marshmoobles by now! I can just imagine his cheeks all puffed out full to bursting crammed with marshmoobles and the tell-tale bit of sticky mooshes dribble!

When I got back to Nanny's I had a nice surprise as Auntie Em and Step Grampy were home, they have been out for a walk too today but not where we went. They were chatting away to William, or more William was chatting at them! He was talking a million miles an hour as he was so excited to see them and tell them all about our journey down and the things he had been up to since he last saw them. He was even forgetting to draw breath as he was so keen to get his words out. They couldn't even get a word in edgeways!

Lou is going to cook something special for tea as it is so long since we have all been together at once. Worryingly Nanny offered to help but we just let her chop vegetables, so it was safe. Nanny isn't much of a cook. She once made a cheesecake that was sweating in the fridge! I think that would be the only cheese related item other than feet that William wouldn't eat! Luckily Nanny didn't try and make a pudding and had bought a salted caramel trifle for pudding and William was straight in there and even licked the bowl clean when it was empty. Lou had to be quick with a towel as he had creamy sticky mooshes and paws and was worried he would get it all over Nanny's house and I don't think that would go down well especially on our first night of our holiday!

We are now snuggled in bed after a hot but extremely exciting first day. Night night!

Sunday 9th August 2020

This morning we went to see Great Nanny. We love going to visit her. She has great stories. I wonder if that is why she is called our Great Nanny? William thinks she is great as she always gives him biscuits, today she presented him with a giant box of mixed chocolate covered biscuits! He worked his way through the box at an impressive speed. Ones with caramel in, ones that crunch when you bite, some even had chocolate chips, my favourite is a classic chocolate finger. I like to chomp in like a little bunny with a carrot. William got himself absolutely smothered in chocolate! It is so hot today and the chocolate was melting faster than even William could eat them!

After we cleaned William up we went back to Nanny's house for lunch. How William could fit lunch in after all the biscuits he ate I just don't know! As we had such a busy day yesterday and Lou says she has planned an exciting and busy day for tomorrow we have decided to relax and play in Nannys garden.

The weather is scorching. We tried to lay in the sun. William made himself very comfy on nannys nice squishy cushioned reclining chair. He made me laugh as he hadnt quite locked it into place and as he sat down it made a loud noise and tipped him backwards! It didn't hurt him but he was stuck on his back with his little legs thrashing around in the air as he tried to put himself right again but the cushion was so bouncy he couldn't get himself up! We were both laughing so hard which didn't help at all as the harder we laughed the more William botty coughed which unbalanced him even more!! Laughing so hard made us even hotter and we decided to go and sit in the shade and have a lolly to cool down.

Nanny came to sit out with us for a bit too. We love getting to spend so much time with Nanny. We still feel like we have a lot of catching up to do as we didn't see her for so long when we were on lockdown and we werent allowed to go out. That time was important though as it meant we were able to protect everyone in the whole world from getting really poorly.

Me again, We have just got back from the beach and it is way past our bedtime, Its actually dark out! That's how late we are! It has been so hot today Lou waited until sunset to take us down. We went looking for crabs in the rock pools and could run around on the sand without burning our toe beans as we chased each other and played.

Looking for crabs was brilliant even though we didn't see any. We clambered over the rocks but they were all covered in slimy cold seaweed. William was slip sliding over rocks and he was so funny to watch. It looked like he was doing an audition for Dancing on Ice! Everytime he took a step one foot went one way and the other foot went in the opposite direction. His arms would fly around like a windmill as he was trying to balance and it looked like he was trying to grab hold of thin air!

While were looking for crabs William was being really noisy. Even noiser that usual and not just because he was slip sliding all over the place. I think this was because he was actually scared as I had joked that a crab would pinch his bum so he was being noisy to scare them off!

We also played chase along the sand. I can run a lot faster than William so when it was his turn to chase me I would go slower and sometimes let him catch me so it was fairer and he could enjoy the game too. I also made sure not to catch him straight away.

We played a balance game along the groyne too. They are quite narrow and covered in barnacles and seaweed its really hard not to fall off as you walk along. We were like the gymnasts you see on a balance beam but we were a lot less graceful!

We watched the sunset and the sky turned beautiful reddy orangey colours. Because it was so hot the air was sort of hazy so as the colours changed in the sky it was like when you wash a paintbrush in water, swirly colours in the clouds. The sunset was very impressive. It was like a picure continually changing. Every time I blinked it looked like the sky was completely new!

It was nice to play now it's a little bit cooler and it is always so good to get down the beach, Sadly at night time the ice cream shops are closed but we have been spoilt today with chocolate biscuits and a lolly at nannys. We walked back to Nannys in the last of the light. We will sleep well tonight I am sure. This little late evening adventure has been the perfect end to the day.

Monday 10th August 2020

Well what a day! It has been amazing!!! It was quite early and straight after breakfast, well straight after we had picked the smooshed banana out of Williams fur and wiped his jammy paws, we hopped on Bobby bike and whizzed along the Sandown to Newport Red squirrel cycle path. We love that route so much as all the flowers are beautiful and there is so much to see and learn along the way and it is a really comfortable ride for Bobby Bike.

We even stopped to pick (and in Williams case, eat) some blackberries. The first time we ever went blackberry picking, Lou explained to us that you should never pick more than you need or plan to eat so that there is enough for everybody and all the birdies and animals to eat too. William takes the "only pick what you plan to eat" bit very seriously as he always plans to eat a lot of blackberries!

When we got to a place called Shide we went on the road and headed through Carisbrooke. We went up a great big hill that felt like a mountain. It was so steep and went on for ages and Lou was puffing away but Bobby Bike did so well and charged up it full steam ahead all the way to the top.
Lou was really sweating by the time she got to the top as we are still in a heat wave. William and I didn't feel puffed out at all!!

Once we had got over the mountainous hill we went along on lovely country roads that everywhere you looked you could see huge fields. Some were farms growing crops and some had animals in like sheep and cows. We had some really fantastic views to look at as Bobby pushed on under the blazing sun. It felt like we could see for 100 miles in every direction, Lou still hadn't told us where we were going.

After a while Lou pulled up into a car park and we saw a big sign for "CHESSELL POTTERY CAFÉ" and we learnt that today's surprise was we were going to be treated to lunch out AND get to paint some pottery!

When we arrived, we were introduced to a nice lady called Charlotte. She explained to us what we needed to do. Our first job was to choose the pieces we wanted to paint. Charlotte explained that the unpainted pottery is called Bisque.
William chose a doggy and I picked a bear like me! He was holding a "B" for Bobtor!

Charlotte helped us choose our paint colours and put them into paint palettes for us and gave us both some paint brushes and a pot of water to clean them. She even gave William a pinny to wear, she must have heard about him! We used our palette to carefully mix the colours to get what we wanted.

We concentrated really hard on our painting. I've never known William so quiet. He even had his little tongue poking out!

We had a lovely egg on toast for lunch as we painted. William was a bit distracted when the food arrived as he was torn between focusing on his painting and his love of food! There was even a moment when he nearly painted his food!!

With William distracted by the food he got all covered with paint. Turns out badgers aren't the best at multitasking! Good job he had his pinny on!

It was such a treat to have lunch out. We went back to our painting after William had hoovered up every crumb left on the plate. Painting is hungry work he says! We were getting to the really tricky parts of our pottery now that required a tiny pointy brush and a steady paw. We had worked so hard it would be a shame to spoil it now by rushing. We took it in turns with the little brush until we were all finished and then Lou put them to one side of the table to dry.

As we had done such a good job on our arty pieces and been so well behaved, we were allowed a giant piece of chocolate cake. William thinks Charlotte chose him the biggest slice as his painting was so good. The cake was delicious. So light and spongey with a rich smooth chocolate cream and topping. There was even a solid chocolate star on top covered in multicoloured sprinkles! William obviously got chocolate all over his mooshes and even up his nose!! So as not to waste the smallest smidgeon of chocolate cake William was trying to lick it of his nose with his tongue! I'm just glad I didn't get any on my nose as I'm sure William would have tried to lick that too!

Charlotte kindly wrapped up our painted pottery once it was dry and made sure it was as well protected as could be. We chose a present to take back for Auntie Loofa at home so she can paint her own and hopefully she will enjoy it as much as we did. Maybe we will even tell her that pottery is best painted with a side dish of chocolate cake!

We had a whizzy cycle back as it was all down hill. We were so fast it was amazing, but we had to be a bit careful as we had precious cargo on board with our pottery. We followed our Red squirrel cycle path all the way back and we went in to see Great Nanny on the way home so we could show her our lovely painted pottery. William kept saying it wrong and accidently told Great Nanny that he had painted a dog potty!! He hadn't realized and couldn't work out why we were all laughing so hard. She was extremely impressed with our hard work.

I think we will be in bed early tonight as we had such a late night yesterday after our trip to the beach and today has been so much fun but has left us quite exhausted.
Once William has finished showing everybody his painting anyway!! He even made poor Katy, Nanny's next door neighbour look as she was trying to hang out her washing!

Tuesday 11th August 2020

William was exhausted after yesterday. I think it is the longest William has ever focused so hard on a non-food item! He has decided to have a lazy day and not do much as he is so worn out. He is going to stay at Nanny's house and have a rest.
I'm sure it is nothing to do with the pile of marshmoobles he has found!
I went on a walk with Nanny and Lou. The weather was still so so hot, but we set out from Nanny's house and headed through Shanklin town towards the Old Village. Its very pretty there with lots of pretty little cottages with thatched roofs. It reminded me of when

we came on holiday before and went to Godshill. There are lots of lovely shops, cafés and restaurants in the Old Village.
As it was so hot, we made sure we packed lots of juice and we were determined to have a lovely walk.

We walked down past the entrance to Shanklin Chine. There was such a quaint little stream that runs across the road there then flows all down through the Chine. The chine is a deep cut through a rock where the water has worn it away for hundreds of years cutting out a grove so the water can flow all the way down to the sea. I haven't walked down through Shanklin chine in a long time but it's quite damp from the spray from the waterfall and so green with big plants and ferns. It feels like you are walking through a dinosaur land or in a jungle. It is like you enter a secret hidden world.

We stomped up a great big hill in a place called Luccombe. We found a fantastic little tea shop that was called "Smugglers Haven" Lou explained to me that a smuggler was someone that would bring things on or off the island without permission.

We were very lucky as the tea shop was just opening when we arrived, and we were already so tired and sweaty after our big climb up the hills we stopped for a mint choc chip ice cream tub. It was real Isle of Wight ice cream that was actually made on the island! It was so delicious and creamy and really well earnt! The mint flavour was so refreshing and exactly what I needed. It was melting quickly in the heat, but I didn't spill a single drop.

After our little rest and snack we carried on walking but we headed down through some trees which was a relief as the shade from the hot sun. It was quite a

dense wood and other than the twigs cracking beneath our feet as we walked you couldn't hear anything.

Well other than Nanny and Lou chatting and laughing of course!

We were walking through an area called the landslip. Lou explained that sometimes there are cliff falls and landslides on the island as the cliffs get eroded but the sea and the weather. Eroded means that it gets worn away. In the landslip is a set of steps called Devils' Chimney.

I've walked through it before with my Grandad. It's a really tight nick in the cliffs with a set of steps through. It was super exciting and felt like a proper adventure. You must really breathe in to get through and I'm not sure after all the marshmoobles that William would have been able to fit! The stone steps are old and well worn so you must be careful not to slip as it would be a nasty tumble down. I made sure I held on tight to the railings with my paws. It was really cool through the chimney, it felt like air conditioning on full blast but that's because the light and heat can't get down there.

I was really surprised as after not long after we left the woods, we found ourselves next to the sea. It was crystal clear and the revetment looked like it stretched for miles. There was so many people enjoying the sea or walking and cycling along there. There were people swimming in the sea. We saw some people walking along with ice creams and that made my tummy rumble. I was really looking forward to our picnic lunch. We were very nearly in Ventnor.

We chose to stop on Ventnor beach for our lunch and we laid out our bright yellow spotty blanket and get out our picnic. It was brilliant watching everyone playing and running in and out of the sea and just have a few minutes to rest our feet. It feels like we have walked a really long way already. Ventnor beach is different to Shanklin as it isn't a sandy beach. It is made up of teeny tiny little stones you call shingle. It was great for when we had our picnic as we wouldn't accidently get sand in our food.

For lunch I had a cream cheese bagel which was still fresh and delicious as Lou had packed ice packs in out lunch box. Whilst we were eating, her and Nanny were using them to try and cool themselves down a bit too!! I don't think they cared that they looked a bit silly, but it really did make me chuckle.

After we finished our lunch we started to head back the way we came with full tummies. We were enjoying the stunning views of the shimmering blue clear sea along the revetment and thoroughly enjoying our day until we realized that all the steps we had happily skipped down to get down to the seafront on the way there we now had to climb up on the way back!

From the bottom we looked up the stairs and there looked like there were thousands stretching all the way up through the clouds into outer space! It was not just because I am so little either. I looked round and Lou and Nanny's faces looked as crestfallen as mine. All of our feet were throbbing as we had already walked so far, and the sun was still blazing and the temperature had reached 34 degrees.
We took deep breaths and began to climb!

Each step felt like climbing a mountain but we were pleased that they had a sturdy handrail and they were in good condition as we used the rail to pull ourselves up and we didn't have to worry about them being slippery. Upwards we marched and we were so proud of ourselves as we got to the top. We stopped at the top and it was amazing looking down and seeing what we had achieved especially where it had been so hard. The view was stunning too.

We were rewarded after our great big climb up the steps as we were back at the "Smugglers Haven" tea shop. We took a quick pit stop for a sit down and a cold drink and an ice lolly. I have been really spoilt today with treats but as it is so hot I need it to keep cool! We sat down on the bench and I had a nice cold can of fizzy pop and an orange fruity lolly. We were so thirsty and had finished all the juice we had packed. The lolly was just as refreshing as the can of pop. Seeing the tea shop at the top of all that climbing was like seeing an oasis in the desert. I was grateful it wasn't a mirage! The views from here and as we walked back down through Luccombe were lovely and we could see for miles.

Poor William was a bit disappointed when I got back to Nanny's and he found out that he had missed out on ice cream AND a lolly but looking at the hot, sweaty, tired state we arrived home in he was glad he didn't come. He really does hate walking!!

I have had such a lovely day with Nanny and Lou and really enjoyed it. We have walked 10 and a half miles which certainly explains why my paws are achy and I'm so very tired. I think I will fall asleep before William tonight as all that fresh air and hard stomping has worn me out. I must have an early night tonight as Lou says she has a really exciting surprise for us tomorrow and a whole day of fun planned again.

Wednesday 12th August 2020

Today was incredible! First, we helped Lou make apple and blackberry crumbles with the fruit we picked earlier in the week ready for Step Grampy's pudding tonight. It seemed to be taking a long time to fill the dish until I realized as I was putting the sugary fruit in William was pinching it back out and munching it!! He is so cheeky. We had only just had his breakfast but that never stops William. Cooking was loads of fun, but little did we know that that was just a taster compared to what was to come.

With the crumbles in the fridge ready for dessert we hopped on Bobby bike and headed out on our favourite route from Nanny's house on the cycle path through to Langridge.

We cycled past the Garlic Farm shop which sent William into a tizz as he really wanted to go in and he thought that was his special surprise. When Lou said we couldn't go in his little eyes filled with tears and his bottom lip started to tremble but Lou said that we would go tomorrow with Grandad for a super duper brunch as today we had something he really wouldn't want to miss.
It's going to take something pretty spectacular to beat a visit to the Garlic Farm in William's eyes!

William thinks the Garlic farm does the yummiest food in the whole world and he loves going into the shop there as it means he can take the yumminess home too. It is such a pretty place. There are some lovely walks around the farm, and I think you can even stay there on holiday. William would love that so much.

We cycled up a great big hill. It was very steep and long. I'm beginning to wonder if all super exciting cool adventures have to involve great big hills!! Lou puffed and panted all the way up and Bobby creaked up under the strain. We were very lucky that the roads were quiet as we were going so slowly like a snail all the way to the top. After the dizzying heights of the giant hill it was then all downhill the other side. We absolutely flew down it the other side. Williams ears were flapping in the breeze as we zoomed along. We must have been going at 30 mph. We free wheeled at great speed all the way to a place called Havenstreet. I love going down hills fast but make sure I am very careful to hold on super tight. Once we had slowed down and the road had levelled out a bit, we started to get closer to a sign and then it came into view clearly, we were at the Isle of Wight Steam Railway!!!

William's eyes nearly popped out of is head when he saw all the old steam trains. He calls them cloud choo choos! Silly William. William loves trains. He has never seen a cloud choo choo in real life before.

Our first stop was the gift shop as William was desperate for a train driver's hat to wear so he could feel like a real train driver. Nanny had given us £5 spends each so we could get ourselves a souvenir each of our holiday and now I know why she saved it until today as Lou had told her where we were going. I got a cool shiny blue badge that says Train Driver on it as not a lot of the clothes and hats fitted me in store. William was made up with his hat. He puffed put his chest and his smile was nearly reaching from ear to ear. I think he is even prouder of his hat than his doggy he painted on Monday. He was marching around like he was the boss.

When we were all kitted out, we headed off to investigate the railway. We didn't investigate for long before we found an ice cream kiosk! Lou treated us to tubs of ice cream, it was so sunny again today and the weather so warm she said we could not be trusted with cones as it was melting so fast!

It was perfect timing because as we were sat eating our ice cream, we were able to watch a train come in and we saw the engineers filling up the water and stoking up the engine. William was absolutely blown away watching the people work. It smelt amazing as the coal was being loaded in the furnace on the engine.

The clouds of steam huffed and puffed from the train and the water fizzled and hissed as it got hotter.

William had managed to get ice cream all over his mooshes as he kept getting distracted by the trains and missing his mouth or dripping it all over himself! I couldn't believe that for the second time in the week food hadn't been William's number one priority.

We made a quick toilet stop to get him all cleaned up again and get the ice cream off him. He wasn't impressed as he was worried, he was missing out on something going on. Lou had barely got him clean before he had dashed out again, still all wet and waddled himself quickly so he could see the trains again.

As we walked around the station, we discovered we were allowed to go into the workshop where they restore the trains and carriages. Restoring means that you take one that is old, and a bit poorly and very carefully make it look good as new! Some of the old carriages looked in a right pickle and we could hardly believe how they could be transformed. It must be extremely hard work and take a long time to mend them. William was eyeing up the tools as he really wanted to help but even though he meant well William is a bit heavy pawed and doesn't know his own strength so being in charge of a hammer anywhere near a delicate old rare train carriage would be a big mistake. Lou and I decided that would only end badly so we hurried him along to the museum!

Inside the museum we had to wear our masks as the dirty horrible virus is still about and some of the exhibits where you press buttons were not allowed because nobody wants to get poorly. We don't mind, it is something to look forward to next time we come.

We learnt all about when they closed a lot of the railway lines on the Isle of Wight and guess what, our favourite cycle path used to be a railway line!! William is sad now that he knows there used to be more trains on the Island as he feels that he missed out. I explained to him that it was a long time ago even before Lou was alive and that if the trains were still running Bobby Bike would not be able to enjoy our favourite cycle path.

We also learnt the history of how the Isle of Wight Steam Railway started. There was so much to see and do still and we were even allowed to look in some of the carriages that had been restored in the workshop we saw earlier.

There was a cool engine so you could see what it was like to be a real train driver and play in. We thought William was never going to leave it and I think he would have happily played there all day as I think when he grows up, he would like to be a train driver. He was making click clack noises and every so often would bellow a "WOO WOO" as loud as he could. He was pulling all the levers and looking at all the dials. He got lost in his own imagination. I don't think he even remembered we were there too.

We really enjoyed the museum and William is now bursting with train facts, makes a change from him bursting with botty coughs!

We toddled back around to the picnic area just in time to see a falconry display by Haven Falconry. It was such a hot day they had to keep the display short and bring out birdies from hot countries. It meant that the birds would be used to the hot weather and not get poorly. We didn't mind that it was a shorter display as we would rather the birdies be safe. A lady was coming round to show us a vulture. Vultures are funny looking. They have bald, wrinkly heads and really pointy beaks. They also have long pointy clawed feet. She put it on our picnic table so we could have a better look. I was a bit scared but when the man was talking, he was telling us all the things they eat but he never mentioned little bears, so I decided that I was safe. They also showed us 4 black kites flying above us. William leaned back to try and look up to watch and he toppled over backwards! He didn't hurt himself or need a plaster, but the shock did cause him to botty cough which of course then had us in fits of giggles!

We soon composed ourselves again when Lou told us it was time to actually ride the train. We felt like royalty going into our beautiful carriage. We had it all to ourselves. William couldn't decide what window he wanted to look out and wanted to see everything at once and didn't want to miss anything, so he was darting from one window to the other and back again. He was overcome with joy that he was on a train and kept giggling and letting out funny little squeaks of excitement. I thought Williams eyes would pop out of his head!

The train chugged along and the track beneath us went click clack whilst the steam was billowing from the engine. It smelt really nice. The train gently and rhythmically rocked side to side. As we looked out the window of the train and looked back, we could see all the other passengers peering out the windows too!

It was wonderfully comfortable in our carriage. The seats were soft and bouncy, and we bobbled along as the train moved. The restoration was amazing. There was the beautiful shiny varnished wood, the posters from back at the time, the fancy lampshades. The whole experience was breath-taking.

The train chuntered on and we went through Ashey station through to Smallbrook station where some people got on who had arrived from the normal train. We went through tunnels and under bridges and some of the bridges we had cycled over to get to the railway in the morning. It went all dark when we went into the tunnels, but we were too excited to be frightened even though the whole carriage went dark and the steam puffed in the windows. We giggled loudly which echoed when we were in the tunnel.

The train tooted its whistle which made us all jump which made William's bum trumpet toot too! We got back to Havenstreet and we thought our ride was over, but it wasn't. It felt like an extra bonus when the train took us the other way down the track, and we headed towards Wootton station. A few people chose to leave the train here as there is a nice walk around the area. William didn't want to leave the train, ever let alone to go for a walk!

Every time the train needed the change in direction the engine would disengage from the carriages and the driver would huff puff it along side us to get to the other end ready to pull us back.

The train then took us all the way back to Havenstreet where we started. We had been on the Cloud Choo Choo for a whole hour. I definitely think this will be William's favourite day of the whole holiday if not ever!

We dragged William off the train, He would have stayed on it all day if he could have. We only managed to lure him away with the news that it was time for lunch! He was still trying to walk half backwards to make sure he was seeing the train as much as possible but it did cause him to knock over a red fire bucket full of water as he wasn't looking where he was going. The metal bucket made a loud clang and water spilled everywhere. The man all dressed up smartly as a conductor on the platform didn't tell William off as he went to apologize and just said he should look where he is going as there will be plenty of time to see more of the trains and that they were going for their lunch too so he promised William he wouldn't be missing out on anything.

We headed towards the picnic area which was where we watched the birds earlier. William was very careful to check there were no birdies out flying around incase they tried to steal his snacks! William ate quickly and messily as he was rushing to get back to where the trains were, but I think he ate a bit too quickly as he was then struck with the hiccups! He is so noisy.

We finished our delicious picnic of cheesey bagels, popcorn, malt loaf and peaches. William was still hiccupping and had a bit of a tummy ache from eating so quickly so we took him for one last look around and to say goodbye to the trains and the nice people and went back to get back on Bobby Bike, William was a bit upset to have to take his train drivers hat off and put his helmet back on but he knows that we need to be safe. We cycled toward Big Rob's house in Ryde. After a while William was feeling better and had stopped hiccupping so William and I were pretending to be trains and making choo choo noises as Bobby flew along. Sadly, Bobby got a bit poorly along the way to Big Robs house and his pedal cracked. It didn't fall off, but it meant Lou has to ride very carefully until we can get him some new ones.

At Big Rob's house William talked nonstop at Big Rob about the trains as he was so excited. Big Rob also loves a visit to the Steam Railway, but he wasn't able to come with us today as he had been working. I don't think he will need to visit for a while as William had told him every single little detail at speed, loudly until he crashed out as he had worn himself out with all the excitement so we just let him have a little sleep. I bet he is dreaming of trains! His little toe beans were twitching as he slept!

We cycled home with William still asleep in the basket riding carefully not to wake him and to look after Bobby Bike's poorly pedal. We got home just as the sun was setting. A tiring but totally incredible day.

Thursday 13th August 2020

We are having a lovely day today. We have been to the Garlic farm as Lou promised William after we had to ride past it yesterday. Grandad picked us up from Nanny's house and we went off in his car. Obviously, the whole journey was William talking at a million miles an hour about yesterday's adventure on the cloud choo choos. Grandad didn't get chance to say much as William didn't let up until we got to the Garlic Farm.

We had brunch at the Garlic Farm. Grandad chose a very fancy full breakfast and we had a super garlicky sausage ciabatta. William made sure he had a taste of everything on everybody's plate. The garlic sausages were really good, big and juicy. William loves sausages loads. I really like mushrooms and the ones we had here were cooked in lovely garlic butter.

It was so delicious; it really is one of our favourite places to eat.

After eating we got to look around the shop and stocked up on all our favorites even though we were only here last month. William was in his element! We even bought some treats in the shop for our friends back home.

As we are on holiday Grandad said it was ok to have ice cream even though we had only just had our breakfast but what he didn't tell us was that it was garlic ice cream!! I wasn't sure about it but William was straight in there. To him ice cream is ice cream! He seemed to be enjoying it so I figured it was safe to try!
Turns out garlic ice cream was an absolute win.

It was chocolatey and garlicky and super creamy. I really liked and was so glad we tried it. They put garlic in everything here. In the shop we even saw some Garlic Beers. I'm actually glad we are too young to try that as I was relieved the ice cream was yummy, but I didn't want to push my luck!
Obviously, there was a lot of mooshes wiping required following the ice cream. Sadly, Grandad now must go to work but Lou says she has an idea for an adventure this afternoon if the weather holds off for us. Grandad is going to give us a lift into Newport.

After a few jobs in Newport and a visit to Nanny at work we got on a bus to Yarmouth. We had our masks on like good boys and enjoyed looking out the window. Yarmouth is out the West of the Island and not too far from Chessell Pottery. It is the mouth of the River Yar. That means it is where the river meets the sea.

We went upstairs on the bus as we hoped we would see a bit more as we sped along.

William loves riding buses as he likes to ding the bell.

When we got to Yarmouth Lou said there was a bit of time before our treat, so we had a look around in the shops and around Yarmouth. It is such a pretty little town. There was a brief but heavy rain shower, but it was only quick and came out nice again after, so Lou said our adventure was still on. She bought some emergency rain ponchos as we hadn't packed our macs and said it was just in case it rained later. William didn't look impressed as they were just clear and not as fancy as his flowery mac. We had a little look in some shops and there are lots of lovely cafes, so we had to try and stop William wandering off and following his hooter. I don't know how he can be hungry after all the food at the Garlic Farm, but William is an eating machine. It wasn't too long until Lou took us back to Yarmouth bus station. We couldn't work out what our treat is as we thought we were going to be going back. We waited a few moments at the bus station and then instead of a normal bus a bus with no roof arrived!

We sat upstairs and Lou put down a rain mac as the seats were damp from the rain earlier, but we didn't mind one bit as the views were fantastic. There was also a commentary which was great. We learnt so much as the bus drove along.

The bus went through Freshwater and Totland and to Alum Bay. It briefly stopped at The Needles Pleasure Park, but we didn't get off as the bus took us up a great big hill to the Needles Old Battery. It's an old fort that was used in the war.

Once upon a time they used to test space rockets here. Grandad told me about it once. We didn't go to the old battery as Lou had a few tricks up her sleeve she said, and we wouldn't have time to do it all. It was very high up on the cliff and the road was all turny and twisty. We could see the famous Needles Lighthouse and the other direction were the cliffs that are really pretty as there are lots of different colours. The lighthouse is so noticeable even in the day light as its red and white striped and stands out on its own at the end of a little line of rocks. It looks little from way up here though. We were so high up, but William and I are brave adventurers.

Our open top bus took us back down the hill and stopped at the Needles Pleasure Park again and this time we got off. It was very busy and bustling with children running around playing, families enjoying snacks and ice creams laughter and happy shouts of excitement. William and I stood briefly trying to take it all in. Lou asked us if we were ready for a real adventure and then took us towards a queue under a sign that said "CHAIRLIFT".

Well if we thought the bus up the cliff felt high, we were mistaken! We were going to ride the chair lift over the side of the coloured cliffs down to the beach below!

It was scary but good. It really is like a chair dangling in the sky that rumbles down slowly over the cliff and down to the beach. We queued up and the chairs are constantly moving round on a big loop. They dangle down from the mechanism above, so you have to stand to one side and as your chair comes past you have to jump onto it sitting down straight away and it carries you off. It was a bit breezy, so the chair lift shook a bit. We were so high, and our toe beans dangled down and so did Lou's legs. We had to be careful not to fidget about too much as it caused the chairlift to sway and creak. We had to make sure to hold on tight as it was high and dangerous if you fell. My heart was pounding inside my chest and I could see Williams eyes wide like saucers. We really did enjoy the chair lift even if it was a bit scary. Lou says it is a big part of the island's tourist history. From the chairlift we looked down and saw all the coloured sands in the cliffs. I have never seen a cliff face like it. The white chalk cliff at Culver is lovely but this one looks like it has all the colours of the rainbow and they are streaked with the different tones. It really does look pretty.

The chairlift went all the way down to the beach and you can get off if you want to and go and explore the beach and even have a boat ride out to the lighthouse but Lou told us we were going to stay on this time as she had one more special surprise for us before we go home. We floated back up the cliff watching the distance between our feet and the ground grow bigger. It was a bit scary on the chairlift as it was so high and not a lot holding you in, but we are so glad we went as it was such an amazing, exciting experience.

Because we were so brave on the chairlift, we got a medal to prove we did it. We love medals. We earnt a big shiny, heavy one when we cycled the length of the UK back in May. This one isn't as big and heavy, but we are enormously proud of ourselves.

The fun had not stopped then though. We had one more surprise treat to come. We filled our own coloured sand shape using the beautiful coloured sands that we saw when we were brave enough to open our eyes on the chairlift.

We went into the sand shop and we chose our bottle then a lady told us what we needed to do and gave us spoons and set us up at our sand station. We had lots of colours to choose from and the bottle we chose had a lovely picture of the needles lighthouse on too so it will make a lovely souvenir of a great day. All the coloured sands we were using to fill our bottle were the ones from the cliff face we dangled over on our chairlift ride.

It was so much fun choosing our colours, taking it in turns with our little spoons and trying to make sure that we had a few layers of each of the colours and we had been warned not to tap the jar as it can ruin the patterns. We were working really hard and concentrating on making it pretty and using our little spoons to get it just right. It was really beginning to look beautiful.

William and I were having so much fun and we were chatting and laughing about our adventures on our holiday and all the fun we have had this week as we worked and somehow William accidently snorted some sand up his hooter. It made him do a great big, loud sneeze but, in his effort, not to knock or bash our jar he managed to blow sand everywhere else. Badger snot and sand makes a kind of cement if you were wondering! It was really funny though. He had managed to get his snotty, sandy cement paste all over himself and in his fur! Lou just laughed at him as he was so pleased that he managed not to ruin the progress we had made on our sand shape! She said she would take him to get cleaned up after we were finished and that he should just enjoy filling his shape and just try not to sniff up any more sand!

Once we had finished putting the sand in the bottle, we took it to a lady who put a special stick inside it and made it even more beautiful with wavy patterns. She also put some water in which made the colours even brighter. She sealed it all up with a special bung in the top so it was safe for us to take home and the sand wouldn't come out everywhere. She wrapped it up for us in tissue paper all nice.

We thoroughly enjoyed our day today and just before we got back on the bus home, we were allowed to choose some sweeties from the shop to keep us entertained on the long bus ride home.

It seemed like a good idea until we realized that as William had been munching his sweeties whilst he was peering out the window, but he had accidently been smearing his sticky dribbly mooshes along the bus window. He just thought it had got foggy which is why he was finding it harder and harder to see. Silly William!

We got back to Nanny and Step Grampy's house and made sure that everyone had a look at our sand shape and our medal.

Friday 14th August 2020

We got up a bit late today as we were tired from all the excitement of yesterday. We needed to get Bobby bike some new pedals today so that he is safe for us to ride home tomorrow.

We cycled through to Newport along our cycle path. We had to be careful as we were worried that his pedal might break completely. It was quite cloudy and overcast today and a lot colder than it has been. We found a bike shop where we were able to get Bobby bike some shiny new pedals and the man even put them on for us. He was very helpful, and kind and we could see that Bobby Bike was feeling so much happier and confident now he had new pedals on.

We decided that to give them a real test drive we would take the lovely green tree lined cycle path through to Cowes and then we could look at the boats look around the town. Cowes is famous around the whole world for sailing races that are held there. There is even a special week called Cowes week which is all about sailing and finishes with a magical firework display. It isn't allowed to go ahead this year as you still aren't allowed too many people together in the same place because that's how the nasty virus spreads.

William would love to come and watch that one year as he is quite fascinated by boats but if he wanted to go on one Lou would need to be sure to get him a life jacket like mine as you need to be safe on the water. I think he is very excited thinking about the party night with all the singing and dancing and watching the fireworks as that would mean staying up way past his bedtime.

We started along the path and were following along the beautiful views of the River Medina, but we had not got far before our good fortune turned and it started pouring with rain. Lou is always prepared, and we pulled over and put our rain macs on.
Not wishing to let the weather win we carried on to Cowes and it wasn't too bad as we were quite sheltered because of the trees but as we came out in the open in Cowes we decided that it was too heavy and cold and we would head back to Newport. It's a shame as we were looking forward to seeing the boats and having a look in the shops as we always seem to be passing through Cowes and never manage to have a good look.

We decided we would go to visit Karen at her café and have a nice warm cuppa and slice of cake whilst we dried out a bit. We had a light and fluffy slice of lemon cake that was homemade. We all know that William is a big fan of all kinds of cake, but this was particularly yum. William thinks that Karen cut him the biggest slice as his fur was a bit damp and he came rustling in wearing his dripping rain mac and she felt sorry for him. We were thoroughly spoilt and even had some hot buttered crumpets.
We were thoroughly stuffed with delicious food by the time we left Café Ninety Three.

Our friend Alan even popped in to say hello as he noticed us enjoying our snack. Luckily, Alan is very clever and didn't try to get a bite of William's cake! We made sure that Alan had a donut, so he didn't feel left out.

After we had warmed up and had our snack, we went to see our lovely friends Jennie and Paul who work with Nanny. It was nice to see them and we chatted for ages. Nanny wasn't at work today, but we liked seeing everybody. William was very cheeky and was trying on sunglasses! We were both spoilt with attention from everyone in the shop and no one minded William putting on the stock. He thinks he is going to be The Spectacle Maker's new model.

It was getting quite late and the weather had dried up for a brief spell so we decided we would head off and try and get back to Nanny and Step Grampy's house before it started raining again. We had a fun ride home racing through the puddles and splish splashing about. We were in our mac so we were warm and dry and enjoying the adventure. We got back but sadly it was time to start packing for going home tomorrow so that we can still manage a little walk and picnic with grandad tomorrow before we ride back.

Saturday 15TH August 2020

With Bobby bike all packed and ready to go we all got up early to cram as much as we can into our last day of holiday before it is time to go.

Sadly it's a bit drizzly and wet out and even though its our last day William still didn't want to come on a walk with Grandad but Nanny said she would take him out in the car to the shops and then to visit Great Nanny. He has already told Nanny that he will require 4 biscuits as he has a long ride home later! He is so cheeky, but he knows that Nanny and Great Nanny will spoil him.

Grandad came to pick me up and we went in the car and parked by the Zoo in Yaverland. Not far from where we finished our walk last Saturday! We started to walk up the great big hill where we stopped for our picnic last week and even though it was raining, we could just about see out to sea. I had my hood up to keep me dry, but it wasn't raining hard it was more a misty drizzle.

We got right to the top, but the fog had come in. We went to go and look at the monument, but we could barely see it through the fog which is funny as it is a giant stone oblong! The monument is near a nice restaurant called Culver Haven Inn as we were up at a place called Culver Cliff. You can see Culver Cliff all the way from Shanklin seafront. It stands out as it is formed from chalk so looks a brilliant bright white. A bit different to the multi coloured cliff we saw Thursday but striking just the same.

Even through the fog I managed to spot the ice cream kiosk at the top of Culver by the monument, William has trained me well and would be so proud of my eagle eye snack spotting. We went and got ourselves a tub of Isle of Wight

banana and honeycomb each. It was so delicious. I think it was the best flavour of the holiday! Delicious and creamy. I wish we could take a giant tub home with us, but it would melt on Bobby Bike on our long ride.

We walked back down Culver Down again but down the opposite side. It was quite steep walking down the hill and where it had been so hot and dry earlier in the week but now so wet the ground was hard and the grass was slippery beneath our feet.

We were walking towards a village called Bembridge. I went there before on my last trip to the island, but we didn't come this way. Our walk took us along enclosed footpaths through trees and suddenly, we came out at a clearing and appeared at

Whitecliff Bay holiday camp. It looks very nice there. I think I would quite like a holiday there. I think I will mention it to Lou!

My tummy was beginning to get a bit rumbly, so we decided to head down towards the beach to put our yellow spotty picnic blanket down. The slipway down to the beach was really steep and slippery as it was so wet. I guess that is how it got its name. It was actually quite scary as it felt like my paws were whizzing away beneath me. Lou and Grandad looked so funny waddling down slowly like penguins. It was worth the dangerous walk (slide) down as we found a great area to plant ourselves for our corned beef sarnies looking out to sea. Even though it was cold and it was raining there was still people playing in the sea!

As we headed back the way we came the fog was clearing so even though we had seen it all before it looked different as we could see more clearly and take in some of the views. There were so many blackberry bushes everywhere bursting with ripe fruit William would have stuffed himself silly if he had been here with us. He loves blackberries so much and you often see him with purple juice all round his mooshes!

We walked back up the big hill towards Culver Haven Inn again but this time I could see the monument so clearly now the fog had lifted. I could not see how tall it was last time or maybe I was just too involved in my ice cream!! It is really high. Grandad was telling me that it was called the Yarborough Monument.

My paws were beginning to get a bit tired so was relieved when Grandad reminded me it was all down hill now all the way to the car. I have enjoyed my walk though and seeing Grandad but I know I will sleep well tonight.

William had a fantastic time at Great nanny's house, and she spoilt him as always. He even had the 4 biscuits that he ordered and I'm fairly sure he must have had a few more judging by the crumbs he was covered in and the amount of jam on his mooshes.

It's always sad to be leaving but we have had a fantastic holiday and been to so many places and seen so many fantastic things. We really are lucky to get the opportunities and adventures. Riding on Bobby Bike and having adventures makes us so happy.

It was still a bit wet on our ride home, but we took poor fully laden Bobby back along our cycle path towards Newport. William saying goodbye to every tree along the way!

From Newport we took the greenway back along the River Medina and then the main road into East Cowes to catch the ferry.
We loved getting to spend so much time with Nanny and Step Grampy and getting to see a lot of Grandad.
This has been such a great holiday and we are so lucky.

There is just a short ride to go back from the docks to home when we get off the ferry shortly. This week has been perfect.

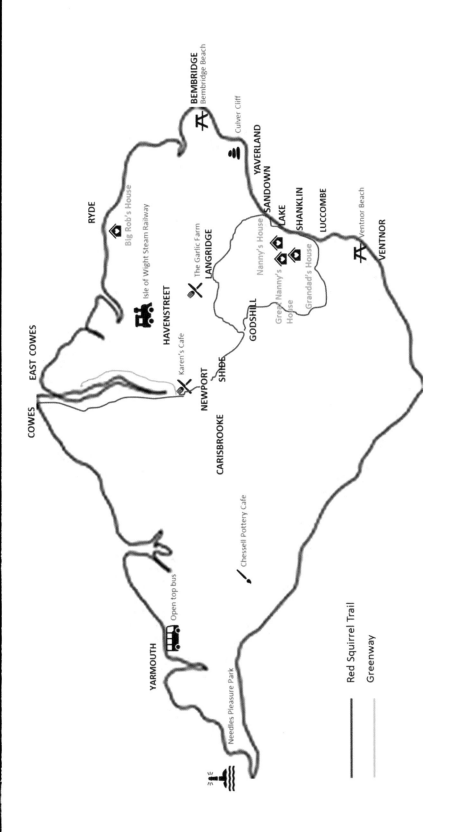

COWES

EAST COWES

RYDE

BEMBRIDGE
Bembridge Beach

Big Rob's House

Isle of Wight Steam Railway

Culver Cliff

YAVERLAND

SANDOWN

LAKE

SHANKLIN

LUCCOMBE

Ventnor Beach

VENTNOR

The Garlic Farm
LANGRIDGE

Nanny's House

Great Nanny's
House

Grandad's House

HAVENSTREET

Karen's Cafe

NEWPORT

SHIDE

GODSHILL

CARISBROOKE

YARMOUTH

Open top bus

Chessell Pottery Cafe

Needles Pleasure Park

Red Squirrel Trail

Greenway

Printed in Great Britain
by Amazon